# Maddy and Mia's Party Business

Story by Pamela Rushby

Illustrations by Rebecca Willoway

# Contents

Chapter 1

# We Need a Business Idea

I was wearing a one-piece dinosaur outfit. It was bright green, with a tail. I had three five-year-old kids hanging off me, clinging closer than koalas, and they were all laughing and squealing and shrieking their heads off. (*At least they're having a good time*, I thought.) And I was doing all this in a park, in public, right in front of a group of the coolest kids in school. What was I doing there?

That's a good question – a *very* good question. It all started with two things: Mr Lee's latest assignment for us at school, and my little sister and brother Daisy and Jake's fifth birthday party.

Every year, Mr Lee's class raises money to help support an animal shelter in our neighbourhood. This year, he had a new idea for how we could do it. We were all happy to help – especially my best friend, Mia, and me. We love animals!

Mr Lee explained. "I want you to work in groups and think of a small business that you could set up to raise some money for the shelter. And I want you to make a business plan."

"What's a business plan, Mr Lee?" I asked.

"Good question, Maddy," said Mr Lee. "A business plan shows how a business will make a profit. All businesses must try to make a profit."

He continued, "Say you decide to sell lemonade at a stall. Your profit is the amount of money you make from selling the lemonade, after subtracting the cost of buying the ingredients and advertising the stall." Mr Lee went on, "So, once you've thought of an idea for a business, you will need to plan how you will advertise it and think about any set-up costs, in order to make a profit."

We all nodded. "Let's work together!" Mia said to me. "We could do something like dog walking, or gardening."

"Or putting the bins out on rubbish collection days for people who can't manage it?" I suggested.

The other kids in the class started organising themselves into groups, too. But then Mr Lee walked up to our table. He had the new boy, Ned, with him. Ned hadn't been at our school for very long.

"You're the smallest group," Mr Lee said to Mia and me. "And Ned doesn't have a group, so I'd like him to work with the two of you."

Mia and I looked at each other. We'd rather have worked by ourselves, but Ned needed a group, so we smiled at him and made room at our table.

"Now, start to think of the kind of business you might run," said Mr Lee to the class. "You have a week to come up with an idea."

Mia and I told Ned about the ideas we'd had. Ned had some ideas, too.

"We could wash cars," he suggested. They were all good ideas, but we could hear that other groups had already chosen most of them. Mia, Ned and I agreed to think of some more ideas over the weekend and talk about them next week.

I walked home, thinking all the way about small business ideas. But when I got home, I forgot all about them at once – because Mum wasn't feeling well.

Chapter 2

# A Plan for a Party

We all sat on the end of Mum's bed: Daisy, Jake and me – but not too close, because we were pretty sure Mum was contagious. Her eyes were red-rimmed and watery. Her nose was red and swollen, too. Her voice sounded as if she was trying to talk from underwater. Her face screwed up and we could see she was trying to tell us something. We leant in closer. What was she trying to say? Was it something really important?

"Maddy, pass me the tissues!"

I passed them.

"Ahh – ahh – ahh – CHOO!"

Mum certainly had a case of the flu, in the worst way. I could see she was feeling terrible. But it wasn't just the flu that was making Mum feel terrible. It was what she had to tell my almost-five-years-old sister and brother.

"I'm sorry, Daisy and Jake," Mum snuffled. "But I'm afraid we'll have to cancel your party." The twins' birthday party was on Sunday afternoon.

There was a moment's horrified silence, before the twins' combined howls filled the air. Then, "No! Not our party!" squealed Daisy.

"Our birthday party? No birthday party?" cried Jake.

Mum grabbed another tissue. "I can't cook for it when I'm like this," she said, sinking back onto her pillow. "And I'm not feeling up to organising games for your whole class. I'd give everyone the flu! I'm so sorry, Daisy and Jake, but we'll have to put it off. Maybe we can have it in a week or so, when I'm feeling better."

Daisy and Jake looked down at their toes. They looked as though they were going to cry.

"But, in a week or so, it won't be our real birthday," said Daisy.

"It won't be the same," Jake agreed. "It'll all be spoiled!"

Mum looked as though she was going to cry, too. "I'm sorry," she said. "But I just don't think I will be up to it."

I looked at Mum, and then at the twins. They were all on the verge of tears. I couldn't bear to see them so upset. "I suppose I can do it," I said.

"You can?" Mum didn't look at all sure about this.

"Sure I can," I said. Actually, I wasn't at all sure I could, but I had to give it a try. "I could ask Mia and her mum to help with the food."

"Will there still be ice cream?" asked Daisy, hopefully.

"And a birthday cake?" asked Jake.

"All of that," I said.

"But who's going to organise the games?" asked Mum.

"We have to have games," said Daisy, firmly.

"Lots of games," said Jake.

"Oh, I'll do that," I said. "I'll get Mia to help me."

Daisy and Jake looked at me doubtfully.

"At Oliver's party, a man came and did magic tricks," said Jake.

"At Bella's party, everyone dressed up like fairies," said Daisy.

"Well, Mia and I will dress up," I said. "How about that? And we'll have games – lots of games!"

"Will you do magic tricks, too?" asked Jake.

*How big do Daisy and Jake expect this party to be?* I wondered. *I can't do magic tricks!* I was ready to say forget the whole thing, when I looked at Mum. I saw how much less worried she was looking, now that she was thinking the twins could have their party after all.

"No magic tricks," I said firmly to Jake. "But Mia and I will dress up as something really cool."

"What?" asked Daisy.

I looked at Daisy and Jake. They were both wearing their one-piece dinosaur outfits. They love those outfits so much.

"Dinosaurs," I said. "We'll dress up as dinosaurs. Dinosaurs will run the party." I knew that a local party shop had one-piece outfits in all kinds of animal designs, and they didn't cost very much. We'd be able to buy dinosaur outfits there, I was sure.

"Dinosaurs?" said Daisy and Jake. They thought about it for a moment. "YES! Dinosaurs!" they yelled.

"Are you sure you can do this, Maddy?" croaked Mum. "It won't be too much trouble? I can text Mia's mum and ask whether she and Mia can help. I'd pay for all the food, of course."

I passed Mum another tissue. "It won't be any trouble," I said.

It was a good thing I had no idea just how much trouble this party was going to get me into.

## Chapter 3

# Daisy and Jake's *Roarsome* Party

Mum sent a text to Mia's mum. Both she and Mia said that of course they would be happy to help. Mia's mum asked me to come to their house the next morning so we could work out what we had to do. But when the twins had gone off to bed happily, I started to worry. Could I really run a birthday party for five year olds dressed up as a dinosaur, even with Mia and her mum's help?

It turned out, I could.

The next morning, I went shopping with Mia and her mum. We bought pizza and little sausages and ice cream and a birthday cake. The lady in the cake shop said she could even put a picture of a dinosaur on the cake, using icing.

Next, we went to the party shop and searched through the racks of one-piece outfits. There were unicorns and cats and dogs and cows and dragons – and yes! Two dinosaur costumes that would fit Mia and me.

"You're lucky," the shop assistant told us. "These are the last two dinosaur outfits we have."

Then, Mia and I went home and made a list of games that we could play with the little kids. We were as ready for Sunday afternoon as we could be.

I'd been worried about us running the party by ourselves, but I needn't have been. It was a big hit! The little kids were thrilled when Mia and I met them as they arrived, wearing our dinosaur outfits.

"Dinosaurs!" they all said. "That's so cool!"

Mia and I kept them running around our backyard playing games, while Mia's mum, with a few other mums and dads who had stayed to help, got the food ready. We had competitions for who could walk the most like a dinosaur, and who could do the best dinosaur roar. Mum was feeling a little better, and she looked out the window to watch the fun from time to time.

At the end of the afternoon, when the parents arrived to pick their children up, the little kids all said they'd had a wonderful time. "It was *awesome*!" they said.

"Don't you mean *roarsome*?" said Mia. The little kids thought that was really funny.

One of the mothers waited after everyone else had left. "I was wondering," she said to Mia and me. "It's my daughter Ava's birthday later this year. Would you girls be interested in running Ava's party?"

Mia and I looked at each other. It had been fun to do the party for Daisy and Jake, but we were feeling really tired. Did we want to do it again?

"I'd pay you, of course," Ava's mother said. "And there's time for you to think about it."

Mia and I looked at each other again. Pay us? Now, that was different.

"Are you thinking what I'm thinking?" I said to Mia.

"I think I am," Mia replied.

So, when we talked about our small business plans at school the next week, Mia and I had an idea to suggest to Ned. When we'd finished talking, Ned looked thoughtful. "You mean a business running little kids' parties?" he said. "Dressed up as dinosaurs? I think that's brilliant!"

"And it doesn't have to be dinosaurs," I said. "The party shop has outfits for dogs or cats or unicorns or dragons. We could dress up as any of those, depending on what the birthday kid wanted. But the dinosaurs were *very* popular."

"The thing is," Mia said, "the shop only had two dinosaur outfits. We wouldn't be able to get a dinosaur costume for you."

"Oh, that's all right," Ned said. "You and Maddy can dress up and run the games, and I'll manage the budget and the advertising and publicity side of it. I don't need to come to the parties."

Mia and I nodded. That seemed fair. So, we started work on our business.

"Our business needs a name," I said. "What should we call it?"

"We could call it Roarsome Parties," Mia suggested.

So we did.

Chapter 4

# Our First Party Booking

Ned had some great ideas for our business. He designed a flyer advertising our parties. Mia drew a picture of a dinosaur and Ned wrote the words: *Make your little dinosaur's birthday party absolutely Roarsome! Let us handle the games and activities for you!* Mr Lee let us make copies on the school photocopier, and we put the flyers in letterboxes up and down the streets. We pinned some up on fences and poles, too. The local shopping centre let us put some flyers on their noticeboards, and the lady in the shopping centre office said she'd put a copy of the flyer on their website, as well.

Ned asked Mr Lee if we could write something about our parties and put it in the school's online newsletter, explaining that our business was raising money for the animal shelter. Mr Lee said we could. Ned thought we needed a photograph to go in the newsletter, so Mia and I dressed up in our dinosaur outfits again, and Ned took some pictures with his mum's phone.

Then, a reporter from the local newspaper phoned to ask us about our business. The newspaper printed a photo of the three of us, sitting around our classroom table – as if we were planning a party. They put it up online, too.

Everything was going beautifully. We'd had several calls on Mum's phone from parents wanting to know more about our parties. Then, there was a call for me, and it was a mother who wanted to make a party booking for her little boy, Rory. I was really excited. It was our first real booking!

"Yes, we can handle that," I told the mother who'd phoned. "Yes, we run all the games, and we can help with food, too, if you would like us to."

"I can do all the food," Rory's mum said. "But I'd love you to organise the games. There's just one thing ..."

"What's that?" I asked.

"Well, we live in an apartment building. We don't have a backyard to hold a party in. But we do have a park nearby. We'd like to have the party in the park."

"In a park?" I asked.

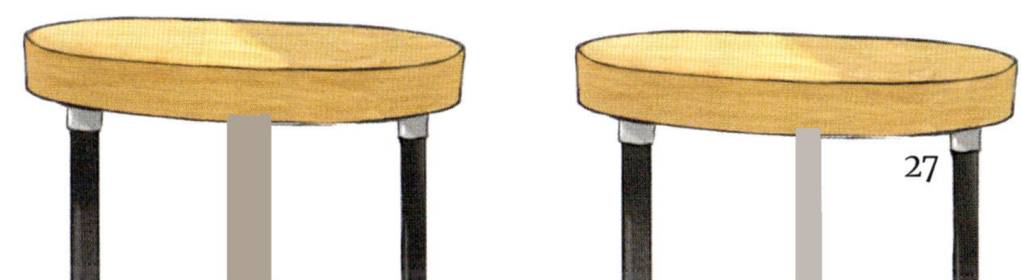

Rory's mum told me which park. I knew the one. It had picnic tables and lots of space for kids to run around. "That's a really nice park for a party," I said. "That's not a problem at all."

But it *was* a problem. And as soon as I told Mia and Ned about our first party booking, Mia let me know exactly why.

## Chapter 5

# Everything Is Not All Right!

"*That* park!" Mia said in horror. "No! *No*! We can't possibly run a party there!"

I couldn't understand her. "Why not?" I said. "It's got picnic tables and there's lots of room. There's even a shelter shed if it rains."

"That's not the problem!" said Mia. "Don't you see? That park is right next to the skatepark!"

"Oh," I said. I hadn't thought of that. I realised what Mia was worrying about now.

"Why does it matter if it's next to the skatepark?" asked Ned.

"Because the skatepark is the place where lots of kids from school go on the weekend," said Mia. "It's where all the *cool* kids hang out."

"And?" said Ned. I could see he didn't understand the problem, but then, he was new at our school.

“Well, there’s absolutely no way I am going to dress up as a dinosaur and run around with a bunch of five year olds in a park, right in front of all the coolest kids in school,” said Mia, firmly. “They’ll all laugh! We’d never hear the end of it! No, that’s it. You’ll just have to cancel the booking, Maddy.”

I thought about what Mia had said. The kids from school would probably all laugh at us. But I’d already told Rory’s mum that we’d run the party. “I don’t know –” I said.

“Maddy, you have to!” urged Mia. “Just say we can’t do it.”

I wasn’t happy, and I could see Ned wasn’t either, but Mia insisted. So, that night, I phoned Rory’s mum. I’d hardly even said *hello*, when she was telling me how excited Rory was about his party. “He just loves dinosaurs,” she said. “He’s been practising his dinosaur roar all day. Here, Rory,” she called, “come and show Maddy how you can roar.”

"ROAARRR!" went Rory down the phone. "Do you know what kind of a dinosaur I am, Maddy?"

"Um, a triceratops?" I guessed.

"Nooo! I'm a Rorysaurus!" said Rory, triumphantly, and he giggled and giggled.

There was no way I could tell "Rorysaurus" that his party was off. Apart from that, Rory's mum was going to pay us, and I really didn't want to let the people at the animal shelter down, either.

I knew Mia wasn't going to be happy when she heard that I hadn't cancelled Rory's party. But I had no idea how unhappy.

The next day, in our business plan meeting at school, I told Ned and Mia. "I just couldn't do it," I said. "Rory's looking forward to it so much."

"All right," said Ned with a smile. "We'll go ahead with it, then!"

But Mia wouldn't have that. "No!" she hissed. "Just *no*! I'm not going to do it! You can go ahead and get laughed at if you like, but I won't do it!"

Mr Lee looked up. "Is everything all right there, Mia? Ned, Maddy?"

Mia got up. "No!" she said. "It's not! It's not all right! I – I don't feel well!" And she rushed out of the room.

"Oh, dear," said Mr Lee. He spoke quickly to Ms Agnella, our classroom assistant, and she followed Mia. Ms Agnella came back after a while, but Mia didn't. She wasn't at school for the rest of the day. She wasn't there the next day, either.

## Chapter 6

# A Huge Success

I didn't know what to do. I'd hoped that Mia would change her mind and help with the party. She was my best friend, and she'd never let me down before, but it didn't look like she was going to give in. I didn't think I could handle a party on my own. And Rory's party was only two days away.

On Friday, I talked to Ned about it. "I just don't think I can run games for twenty little kids all on my own," I said. "It's going to be a disaster!"

And to be honest, Mia had started me thinking. I was a bit worried about what the kids at the skatepark would say, too.

"Hmm. I guess I'll just have to help out, then," said Ned.

"You don't mean – you'll come and be a dinosaur?" I said. "But you don't have a costume."

"I could wear Mia's, couldn't I?" said Ned.

I looked at Ned. He was bigger than Mia. "The costume will be short and tight on you," I said. "It'll look funny."

"So, I'll look funny," said Ned.

"But what about the kids at the skatepark?" I worried. "Doesn't that bother you? What if they laugh at us?"

"What if they do?" said Ned. "Just think, we'll be the ones raising money for the animal shelter. They won't. I'll bet they won't laugh if they find out we've raised the most money."

I wasn't so sure about that. But I was ready to take all the help I could get.

On Sunday afternoon, Ned and I were at the park early. We helped Rory's mum and dad set out the party food on one of the picnic tables. Rory ran around us in little circles. He was so excited.

"Where are your dinosaur outfits?" he kept asking. "Are you going to get dressed up now?"

"Soon," I said.

I'd hoped there wouldn't be any kids at the skatepark today, but of course there were. When I peeked over, I could see some of them were from our school. *Oh no*, I thought. *I just know they're going to laugh.*

"The children will be arriving any minute," said Rory's mum, hanging up some streamers.

"Time to suit up," said Ned. He pulled on Mia's dinosaur outfit. It wasn't easy for him to get it on. The sleeves came halfway to his wrists. The legs didn't reach his ankles. He could barely do the zip up. It did look strange – but it would have to do.

I couldn't put it off any longer. I pulled my dinosaur outfit on over my shorts and T-shirt. Rory was delighted. "Now you're a Maddysaurus!" he shouted.

"And I'm a Nedosaurus," said Ned. "A *ferocious* Nedosaurus. Watch out!"

Ned growled and pretended to chase Rory, and Rory ran, shrieking with delight.

The kids at the skatepark all looked over to see what was happening. *Of course they would*, I thought.

"They're *looking* at us!" I hissed to Ned.

"Forget about it," Ned said. "Look, some little kids are arriving. Let's get this party started!"

After that, I was too busy to bother much about the kids at the skatepark. I had games to organise. I was amazed at how good Ned was with the little kids. He stomped around like a dinosaur, and roared, and took part in all the games – and always got them wrong, which made the little kids laugh. They just loved him.

"How do you know what will make them laugh?" I asked him.

Ned grinned. He looked like he was having fun. "I used to help with the kids' classes at the surf club where I lived before we moved here," he said. "This party is a lot like that – except these kids aren't as wet!"

From time to time, I snuck a quick look at the skatepark. The kids from our school were still watching us, but I didn't have much time to worry about them. And the party was a huge success!

When Rory had blown out the candles on his birthday cake and all the food was eaten, the little kids started to go home. I was exhausted. Ned looked worn out, too. We flopped down on the grass, not even bothering to take our dinosaur outfits off.

Ned turned his head to one side. "Don't look now," he said. "But we have some visitors."

I looked up. Oh, *no*. The kids from the skatepark were walking towards us. I knew them from school: Alex and Georgia and Blake and Shona. All the cool kids.

## Chapter 7

# Awesome Parties!

I gritted my teeth. What were all the cool kids going to say? Did they come over here to laugh at us?

"Hi," said Ned casually, sitting up.

"Hi," Alex said. "Hey, that was …"

*Here it comes*, I thought.

"… awesome," Alex finished. "Just awesome!"

"Those little kids were having so much fun!" said Georgia.

I stared up at them. They weren't laughing. They weren't teasing us. They thought our dinosaur party was awesome!

Ned was explaining to them what the party was all about. "It's to raise money," he said.

"So, you get paid to do this?" Blake asked.

"Yeah," Ned said. "But the money's for the animal shelter. It's our business plan project, for school."

The cool kids sat down on the grass beside us and we told them all about our party business.

"That's a great idea," Shona said. "I'm doing a business plan, too, but my group's just baking biscuits to sell. That's all right, but this looks like a lot more fun." She hesitated. "I don't suppose – well, would you have room for some more dinosaurs? To help you run the parties?"

"I'd like to do that, too!" The other kids nodded their heads.

Ned and I looked at each other and grinned. We'd had more enquiries from other parents interested in dinosaur parties. We could certainly use more help running them. "We'll think about it," I said.

The next day at school, everyone was talking about dinosaur parties. We were famous! We had kids coming up to us all day, asking if they could join us as well. I couldn't stop smiling. I felt relieved and happy our party had gone so well, but I was still worried about one thing. Mia was back at school that day. What would we say to each other?

Mia didn't speak to me at all in the morning. Our eyes met a couple of times, but then one of us would look away quickly or pretend to be busy with something else. But after lunch, we had a business plan meeting. Mia slowly came over and joined Ned and me at our table. None of us said anything.

Then, Mia said softly, "I'm sorry."

There was silence for a while.

"I – I heard how the party went," Mia said. "All the kids are talking about it. Could I – well, could I be in the group again? And help with the parties?"

I stared at Mia. She'd said she was sorry, and she wanted to join in again. But what would she have been saying if the other kids had laughed at us, I wondered? What if they'd teased us about our dinosaur outfits, and about playing with five year olds? I had to ask Mia that.

"What if they'd laughed at us?" I asked. "Would you want to rejoin our group then?"

Mia looked down again. "I – I don't know," she said. "But I really am sorry."

Mia looked as though she was going to cry. I thought I might cry, too. We'd been friends for so long. But … I didn't know what to say.

"Look," said Ned at last. "You two will have to work out if you're going to be friends again or not, but we've got a business to run." He waved some pieces of paper at us with phone numbers on them. "We have enquiries for several parties here, and they're not all for dinosaurs. We've got other kids wanting to help us run them. I can't do it by myself. So, both of you, are you in? Or out?"

Mia and I looked up. Ned's words sounded promising. Very promising.

"Several enquiries? Not all for dinosaurs?" I asked.

Ned looked at the pieces of paper. "Someone would like a cat party," he said. "And someone else wants pirates."

"Maybe we could do unicorns," said Mia, excitedly. "Or dragons!"

"That's a good idea!" said Ned.

*Well, it looks like Mia's back in*, I thought. And I realised I felt happy about that. I liked it much better when Mia and I were friends. I smiled at Mia, and she smiled back.

"If we're going to do cat parties, and pirates, and unicorns," I said, "we'll need a new name. Cats and unicorns don't roar, so we can't be Roarsome Parties."

"So, we'll be Awesome," said Ned. "Awesome Parties!"

I smiled at Ned and Mia. "And I bet we'll make the most money for the animal shelter out of the whole school!"